D1385185

To Kate

From Hung Phan
&
Nga Nguyen

Best wishes & Good luck in school
God bless you Always.

9/1/94

[signature]

Nga Nguyen

HPhan

Classic Fairy Tales

Retold by Helen Cresswell

Illustrated by Carol Lawson

An Artists and Writers Guild Book

Golden Books
Western Publishing Company, Inc.
850 Third Avenue, New York, N.Y. 10022

For GML

First published 1993 by HarperCollins Publishers Ltd, London.

 ISBN : 0-307-17503-0
Printed in Italy A MCMXCIV

Library of Congress Cataloging-in-Publication Data

Cresswell, Helen.
Classic fairy tales / retold by Helen Cresswell : illustrated by Carol Lawson.
p. cm.
Contents: Sleeping Beauty—Goldilocks—Cinderella—
The Frog Prince—Rapunzel—Snow White and Rose Red—Hansel and Gretel—
Little Red Riding Hood—Snow White and the seven dwarfs.
$12.95
1. Fairy Tales. [1. Fairy Tales. 2. Folklore.] I. Lawson, Carol, ill. II Title.
PZ8. C864At 1994
398.21—dc20
[E] 93-1395
CIP
AC

Contents

~ Sleeping Beauty ~

There once lived a king and queen who were married for many years without having any children. When at last a daughter was born to them, they were so delighted that they gave a feast for the baby's christening. Invitations were sent to all the lords and ladies in the land and to far-off kings and queens.

Thirteen fairies lived in this kingdom, but the king had only twelve golden plates to set before them, and so he had to leave one of the fairies out.

On the day of the christening the king and his guests feasted merrily, and in the evening before they left, each of the fairies presented the princess with a magic gift. One gave her the gift of wisdom, another the gift of beauty; a third wished her all the riches she desired. And so it went until the eleventh fairy had spoken, when suddenly the glittering crowd of guests parted and between them strode the thirteenth fairy, all in black. She looked neither left nor right and greeted no one. She stopped by the side of the baby's cradle, lifted her arms like great black wings, and cried in a terrible voice, "When the princess is fifteen years old, she shall prick herself with a spindle and fall down dead!"

She lowered her arms, and in the great silence that followed, turned and went out of the hall.

Now, the twelfth fairy still had not made her gift. It was beyond her power to undo the wicked spell, but she was able to soften it by saying, "When the princess pricks herself with a spindle, she shall not die, but fall into a deep sleep lasting a hundred years."

Even this seemed a tragedy to the king and queen, and they gave orders that all the spindles in the land should be burned. As the princess grew up, becoming wiser and lovelier and kinder each day, the fairy's curse began to seem very faint and far away, so that they hardly thought of it at all.

On the princess's fifteenth birthday a party was held at the palace. The princess begged for a game of hide-and-seek. The guests scattered, and the princess herself began to run up and down the stone corridors, looking for a hiding place. At last she came to a crumbling tower that she had never noticed before.

"They will never find me here!" she thought.

She climbed the narrow, winding stairs and came to a door with a great rusty key in the lock. The princess turned the key and went inside.

There an old woman sat with a spindle, spinning flax. The princess stared. All the spindles in the kingdom had disappeared long ago, because of the fairy's curse, and so she had never set eyes on one before.

"Good day, Granny," said the princess. She had quite forgotten the game of hide-and-seek. "What are you doing?"

"I am spinning," replied the old woman, nodding her head.

"And what is this that whirls round so merrily?" asked the princess. With these words she reached for the spindle. But she had scarcely touched it before she pricked her finger. The curse was fulfilled. The princess fell fast asleep, and the old woman (who was really the thirteenth fairy) went away down the stone stairs, with her evil laughter echoing about her.

At the very moment that the princess fell asleep, her guests, too, closed their eyes and slept just where they happened to be – some in cupboards, some behind pillars, and others

CL

on top of the great four-poster beds. Even the king and queen fell asleep in the great hall. Their courtiers yawned and rubbed their eyes and soon were sprawling on the strewn rushes. The horses lay sleeping in the stables, the dogs in the yard, the doves on the roof, the flies on the wall. Even the fire on the hearth stopped its flickering, and the meat on the spit stopped crackling. The cook, who was about to box the scullion's ears, began to snore, with her arm still raised for the blow. Outside, the wind dropped. Not a bough stirred, not a twig, not a leaf. All slept.

Around the castle a hedge of briers began to grow up. It grew higher and deeper, minute by minute, until it surrounded the whole castle with live green walls of thorn and bramble. Soon nothing could be seen from the outside world – not even a turret, not even a flag on the roof. Within, the clocks ticked to a standstill, the dust settled, and there was nothing but sleep and silence.

A legend grew up as years went by about the sleeping Brier Rose, as the princess was called. Princes came from far-off lands to try to force their way through the high thicket. But the greedy thorns clutched them like hands so that they could never escape and were left there to die.

Then, one day, when the hundred years were nearly up, a bold and handsome prince rode by. In the woods he met an old man who told him the legend of the beautiful sleeping princess. He begged the prince not to try to enter, warning him of the terrible fate that had befallen the rest.

"I am not afraid," replied the prince. "I am determined to go and see Brier Rose with my own eyes."

He rode to the thicket, never knowing that this very day the one hundred years were ended and the princess would wake from her spellbound sleep. As the prince drew near, he saw to his astonishment that the hedge was covered with large and beautiful flowers. The flowers seemed to be unfurling their petals even as he watched. As he rode up, the briers curled back and made way for him so that he could pass unharmed, and then closed up again into a hedge behind him.

In the courtyard the prince found brindled dogs lying asleep, noses on paws. He saw doves on the roof, heads under wings. He pushed the door and entered the silent palace. There he saw the king and queen themselves, lying by the throne. The prince had to step over the sleeping forms of guards and courtiers before he passed through the kitchen, where the cook had stood for a hundred years with her arm raised ready to box the scullion's ears. Nearby sat a maid who had been fixed in time while she plucked the black feathers from a fowl on her knee.

The prince went on tiptoe through the palace, and so great was the hush that he could hear his own breathing. Then at last he came to the chamber where Brier Rose lay sleeping.

The princess looked so beautiful lying there that the prince knelt by the bedside and gently kissed her.

And to his wonder Brier Rose opened her eyes and gazed up at him. Then she sat up and yawned. She stretched and asked the time of day for all the world as if she had woken from a nap.

The prince and Brier Rose went down together and found the whole palace astir. The hounds sprang up and wagged their tails, the doves on the roof stretched their wings and fluttered off to the fields. The flies buzzed, the fire leapt, the meat began to roast. The scullion received at last the box on the ears that had threatened him for a hundred years, and let out a yell that woke the maid who was plucking the fowl.

Everything went on as if nothing had ever happened, as if a century were no more than the twinkling of an eye. And soon the dust of a hundred years was flying in clouds through open doors and windows as the palace was prepared for the wedding of Brier Rose and her gallant prince.

Goldilocks ~and the~ Three Bears

Once upon a time a family of bears lived in a house in a wood. There was a Great Big Bear (who was the father), a Middle-sized Bear (who was the mother), and a Wee Small Bear (who was the baby). They were very good bears, and the Green Huntsman, who kept the forest for the king, often gave them honey from the wild bees' nest when there was some left over.

One day Mother Bear made some porridge, which was their favorite dish. It was too hot to eat, and because they did not like to sit looking at it as it steamed deliciously in their bowls, they set off for a short walk in the wood.

"When we come back, it will be just right to eat," said Mother Bear.

No sooner had they gone than a little girl called Goldilocks came wandering by, picking flowers. She saw the little house and went to the door and knocked. There was no reply, of course, and as the door was standing a little way open, she gave it a push and went inside. The first thing she saw was the table set with the steaming bowls of porridge.

"I'll sit down and try some," she thought.

"Nobody seems to want it, and it seems a pity to waste it."

Goldilocks sat on the biggest chair, but it was too big. She tried Mother Bear's chair, but that was still too big. Then she sat on the wee small chair, and *crash*! – the leg broke, and the chair and Goldilocks went tumbling to the floor.

"Oh, dear!" said Goldilocks. But she was still determined to try the porridge, so she went all around the table, tasting from each bowl.

First she tried the bowl belonging to the Great Big Bear – because that one was the biggest. It was too hot. So was the porridge in Mother Bear's bowl. But when she came to the last one, belonging to the Wee Small Bear, it was just right, and she ate it all up. She had not *meant* to eat it all, but it was so delicious that she went on tasting and tasting until it was all gone.

"I'm tired now after my long walk," said Goldilocks. "I must find somewhere to rest."

She went upstairs and lay on the bed belonging to the Great Big Bear, but it was too big. Then she tried Mother Bear's bed, but that wasn't right, either. But when she lay on the Wee Small Bear's bed, it felt exactly right, and she was so comfortable that soon she was fast asleep.

Not long after, the three bears came home from their walk.

"Someone's been sitting in my chair," growled the Great Big Bear in his great big voice.

"Someone's been sitting in my chair, too," said Mother Bear in her soft mother voice.

"Someone's been sitting in my chair and broken it all to pieces!" cried the Wee Small Bear in his small shrill voice.

"Someone's been tasting my porridge," growled the Great Big Bear in his great big voice.

"Someone's been tasting my porridge, too," said Mother Bear in her soft mother voice.

"Someone has been tasting my porridge and has tasted it all up!" cried the Wee Small Bear in his small shrill voice.

Then the bears went upstairs.

"Someone has been lying in my bed," growled the Great Big Bear in his great big voice.

"Someone has been lying in my bed, too," said Mother Bear in her soft mother voice.

"Someone has been lying in my bed, and here she is!" cried the Wee Small Bear in his small shrill voice.

Just then Goldilocks awoke. She saw the big furry faces of the three bears looking down at her, and with a loud shriek she jumped up and rushed down the stairs and out of the cottage with her hair flying out behind her.

"She is afraid of us!" laughed the Great Big Bear in his great big way.
"She is afraid of us!" laughed Mother Bear in her soft mother way.
"She is afraid of us!" laughed the Wee Small Bear in his wee shrill way.
As for Goldilocks, she didn't stop to draw breath until she was safely home again.

And she never again went into a house when she found the door standing open, because for all she knew, those three bears might have gobbled her up. How was she to know that they liked only porridge and honey?

~ Cinderella ~

There was once a man whose first wife had died, and so he married again. He did not pick so well the second time. His new wife was spiteful and bad-tempered, and to make matters worse, she had two daughters who took after her.

This man had a daughter himself. She was kind and gentle and beautiful. The stepmother and her daughters were thoroughly jealous of her, and after the man died, they set about making her life as miserable as they could.

They gave the girl all the dirty work in the house. She scrubbed and scoured and dusted all day long while her new sisters sat polishing their nails or admiring themselves in the mirror. They wore jewels and silks and satins while their poor sister had only a few rags to cover herself with. They slept on soft feather mattresses, deep and warm, while she shivered on straw in the drafty attic.

The girl patiently worked and shivered and half-starved without saying a single word of complaint to anyone. At the end of the day when all the work was done, she would sit huddled among the cinders in the chimney corner of the kitchen, trying to keep warm. Even this did not make the ugly sisters sorry. Instead, they laughed and gave her the nickname of Cinderella.

One day many years later the king of all the land gave a great ball for his son, the prince. The stepmother and her daughters were invited, and were soon busily planning what they

would wear and how they would dress their hair.

While the two ugly sisters posed before their mirrors, trying on sashes and twirling their hair into ringlets, Cinderella was sent rushing hither and thither to fetch and carry, to sew and press, so that everything would be ready on the night of the ball. Instead of being grateful for her help, the two sisters mocked her.

"How would you like to go to the ball, Cinderella?" they asked.

"Oh, I would!" she said wistfully. "But people would only laugh. Look at me, in my old rags!"

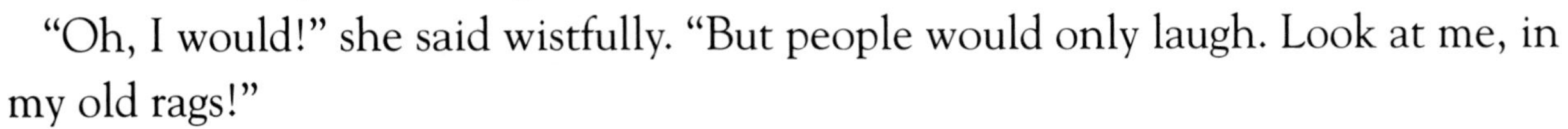

"Laugh? I should think they would!" cried the two sisters. "A fine sight *you* would be at the king's ball!"

On the great day Cinderella worked harder than ever before in her life, trying to send her sisters off to the ball looking their very best. And when the last bow was tied and the last ringlet curled, they *did* look their very best – though even that was not saying very much.

Off they went with a proud flurry of rustling skirts, out to the waiting coach, with not so much as a wave of the hand to Cinderella, let alone a thank-you. When the sound of the carriage wheels had died away and she was alone at last in the great, empty house, Cinderella crept back to her usual place by the hearth and began to cry.

After a while she heard a knocking at the door and, drying her eyes, went to answer. In stepped a little old woman who looked like a beggar in her tattered cloak.

"Why are you crying, child?" asked she.

"Because . . . because . . ." Cinderella did not want to say why she was crying.

"You need not tell me," said the old lady surprisingly. "I know quite well why you are crying. It is because you want to go to the ball."

Cinderella stared at her.

"I am your godmother," explained the other. "Your fairy godmother. And now, child, there's work to be done. Go out into the garden and fetch a pumpkin, quick!"

Cinderella was out in the garden searching for a pumpkin before she even had time to think. When she brought one back, her godmother rapped it smartly with a long black stick – or was it a wand? – and there in a trice stood a golden carriage! It winked and glittered and shone bright as the sun itself.

"Two mice!" ordered the godmother, without a blink.

Cinderella opened the pantry door, and as two mice came scampering out – *poof*! A wave of the magic wand and they were high-stepping horses with flowing manes and rearing heads.

"What about a coachman?" murmured the godmother. "Run and fetch the rattrap, will you?"

Cinderella did not wait to be asked twice. Off she ran, and the next minute there stood a stout coachman with brass buttons and a large three-cornered hat.

"If you look behind the watering can beside the well," the godmother went on, without so much as the twitch of an eyebrow, "you will find six lizards. We could do with them, I think."

Sure enough, there were six lizards exactly where she had said, and a flick of that busy wand transformed them instantly into six tall footmen with dashing liveries.

"Well!" exclaimed the fairy godmother then. "That carriage could take a *queen* to the ball. Do you like it?"

"Oh, it's beautiful!" cried Cinderella. "But Godmother, I still can't go to the ball!"

"And why not?"

"My dress! Look at me! Whoever saw a sight like this at a king's ball?"

"That is easy enough," replied the old lady. "Stand still a moment, child, and shut your eyes."

Cinderella stood quite still, her eyes tight shut. There was a slow cool rustling, a breath of scented air, a soft silken brushing, and then – "Open!" commanded that thin, high voice.

Cinderella opened her eyes.

"Oh!" she gasped. It was all she could say. "Oh!"

About her billowed the most beautiful dress she had ever seen. It was sky-blue, stitched with pearls and threaded with silver. And there, beneath the hem of her skirt, glittered a pair of shining crystal shoes.

"Glass slippers!" gasped Cinderella.

"Off you go now, child," said her godmother briskly. "Off to the ball and enjoy yourself!"

Cinderella gathered up her shimmering skirts and stepped into the golden coach. The footmen bowed. The coachman lifted his whip.

"Wait!" cried the godmother.

Cinderella put her head out of the carriage window.

"Home by twelve sharp! Do you hear? Not a minute later!"

"I shall be back," promised Cinderella.

"Listen for the clock," warned her godmother. "Not a single moment after the last stroke of twelve. If you're even a second late –"

"What?" cried Cinderella in alarm. "What will happen, Godmother?"

The old lady waved her arms.

"*Poof*! Gone! Coach to pumpkin, horses to mice, coachman to rat – *poof*! Gone! Gone! All of it!"

"I'll remember," cried Cinderella. "I promise. The last stroke of twelve! Good-bye, Godmother! And thank you!"

She had a last glimpse of her godmother's shabby figure, and then the coach was rolling

on its way. She, Cinderella, was off to a king's ball!

When at last the golden coach reached the palace gates, the news quickly spread that a great lady, certainly a princess, had arrived. Servants ran to bow and open doors and make a way for Cinderella through the crowds of staring guests. For she was so beautiful that all the people stood quite still to watch her as she passed, and even the music faded as the fiddlers laid down their bows in wonder.

The king's son himself watched her walk among the whispering guests. He went to greet her – and was in love before he had even reached her side. He led her onto the floor to dance, and the fiddlers picked up their bows again and began to play.

All evening long the two of them danced together. The prince could not bear to leave Cinderella's side for even a moment. The other guests were filled with envy and curiosity, and the two ugly sisters were angriest of all.

"Whoever can she be?" they cried, craning to peer at her each time she whirled by. Not for a single minute did they suspect that the beautiful stranger was none other than their sister, Cinderella.

Cinderella herself was so happy that she forgot all about the time. The great ballroom clock was already beginning to chime the hour of midnight when she suddenly remembered her godmother's warning and her own promise to be home by twelve.

"Oh!" she cried. "I'm late! The time!"

Before the astonished prince could collect his wits, she had darted off and was out of the ballroom and running down the great marble staircase to her waiting coach.

Six . . . seven . . . eight . . . the bell was chiming.

The coach clattered away out of the palace courtyard. At the top of the staircase the prince stood looking left and right for a sign of his

vanished dancing partner. He sent the servants to search and they ran all through the palace, but in vain. She had gone. But there, lying halfway down the stairs, was a tiny glass slipper – Cinderella's. Sadly the prince picked it up and wandered away. He did not dance again that night.

Meanwhile Cinderella was hardly out of the palace gates when – *poof*! The spell was broken. All in a moment she found herself out on the empty road. Of the shining coach, the footmen, and the coachman, there was not a trace. From the corner of her eye she saw, running over the road, a thin dark shape, which might have been a lizard. And that was all. Clutching her thin rags about her, she set off for home. Safely there, she climbed up to her cold attic and fell asleep, dreaming of the ball and the handsome prince.

The prince himself did not sleep at all that night. He paced up and down in his room, clasping the glass slipper.

"I must find her," he said out loud. "And when I have found her, I shall marry her and make her my princess."

Next day the prince called the royal herald.

"Come with me," he commanded. "We will search the length and breadth of the kingdom to find the young lady whose foot this slipper fits. For she is the one I will marry."

Soon the news spread about the town. The king's herald went from door to door reading his proclamation and trying the slipper on one foot after another. He had not known there were so many feet in the world. Then at last he and the prince came to the house where the two ugly sisters had been eagerly awaiting his visit, their hair tightly curled and their legs trembling with excitement. One of them, for sure, would fit her foot into the glass slipper and become the prince's bride.

They heard a loud knocking on the door, and the notes of the herald's trumpet.

"Quick!" hissed their mother. "Sit down and look as if you weren't expecting him. And make sure one of you gets that slipper on!"

With that, she sent a servant to open the door, and next minute they were all curtsying

CL

to the king's messenger.

The two ugly sisters tried with all their might to fit their great feet into that dainty slipper. They squeezed and tugged and twisted and muttered and groaned, but all in vain. At last, sulky and red-faced, they gave up the attempt, trying hard not to catch their mother's eye.

"Is there no other young lady in the house?" asked the herald. "I have orders to miss not a single one, whoever she is."

"No!" cried the three ladies together. "There's no one else!"

But it was too late. The herald had already opened the door of the kitchen, and he saw Cinderella sitting there. He bowed politely and offered her the slipper. She held out her foot – and it slid in smoothly.

"It fits!" cried the ugly sisters together. "It can't! It's a trick!"

Cinderella smiled, and taking from her pocket the other slipper, placed it on her other foot. And at that moment her fairy godmother appeared and, with a touch of her magic wand, transformed Cinderella's rags into a snow-white bridal gown.

Only then did the prince recognize her as the beautiful stranger at the ball. The ugly sisters and their mother hurried off, afraid of what might happen to them when their wickedness was discovered.

But Cinderella forgave them willingly, and she drove off with her prince in the king's own coach. They were married that very same day and lived happily ever after.

~ The Frog Prince ~

One evening a young princess went into a wood and sat down under a lime tree by a spring of clear water. She had taken with her a beautiful golden ball and kept tossing it idly into the air and catching it again.

Each time she threw it, the ball rose higher and higher. At last the princess threw it too high and too far, and she missed catching it as it fell. It began to roll away from her, away and away, and before she could reach it, the ball had rolled right into the spring itself.

"My ball! Oh, my ball!" cried the princess in dismay.

She went and leaned right over the edge of the spring, but the water was very deep and she knew that she could never reach the bottom of it. The princess began to cry, because she had really loved her golden ball and could not bear to think that she would never play with it again.

"I loved it best of everything in the whole world," she sobbed. "And I'd give anything – everything I own – to have it back again. All my jewels, all my fine clothes – everything!"

As she finished speaking, a frog suddenly put its flat green head out of the water and asked, "Princess, why do you weep so bitterly?"

"Oh, frog, I have lost my golden ball!" she cried. "It has fallen into the spring, and now I shall never see it again!"

"You *may* see it again," replied the frog, "if you let me help you. I heard what you said

just now. I do not want your jewels or your fine clothes. But if you will love me, and let me live with you, and eat from your little golden plate and sleep upon your bed, then I will bring you back your ball again."

He sat with his green head cocked and looked at the princess with his great round eyes, and she looked back at him.

"What nonsense he talks!" thought the princess. "How could he possibly climb out of the spring? And as for coming to live with me at the palace – it's impossible! But he may be able to dive down and fetch my pretty ball, so I'll pretend to promise what he asks."

"Very well, frog," she said out loud. "I will agree to what you ask. And now, dive and fetch me my ball – quickly!"

So the frog splashed down into the water and disappeared. A moment later he came up again with the ball in his mouth.

"Oh, thank you!" cried the princess, overjoyed. "My ball – my beautiful ball!"

She picked it up and ran gaily off toward the palace, quite forgetting the frog and her own promise.

"Princess, wait!" called the frog. "Remember what you promised!"

But the princess kept on running, and soon she was safely home, her adventure forgotten.

Next day the princess was just sitting down to her dinner when there came a strange, soft pattering noise, as if slippered feet were coming up the marble staircase. This sound was followed by a gentle knocking at the door, and a voice said:

"Open the door, my princess dear,
Open the door to thy true love here!
Remember the promises the two of us made
By the fountain cool in the greenwood shade!"

The princess ran to the door and opened it, and there sat the frog, whom she had quite forgotten! The sight of him frightened her so much that she slammed the door in his face and hurried back to her seat. The king himself was sitting at the table.

"Who was that at the door?" he asked.

"Only a nasty frog," replied the princess. "My golden ball fell into the spring yesterday, and he fetched it out for me. But he made me make a silly promise – to let him come here and live with me – and now he wants to be let in!"

As she spoke, the frog knocked at the door again and sang his sad song:

"Open the door, my princess dear,
Open the door to thy true love here!
Remember the promises the two of us made
By the fountain cool in the greenwood shade!"

"You must let him in," said the king. "If you made a promise, you must keep it. Open the door."

Much against her will the princess went and opened the door. The frog came hopping in and went right over to the table.

"I am hungry," he said to the princess. "Pray lift me onto the table so that I may sit by you."

She did as he asked, though she could hardly bear to touch him. And when she herself had sat down again, he said, "Push your plate a little closer to me so that I may eat out of it."

The princess was forced to obey, though she did not at all like the idea of sharing her plate with a frog.

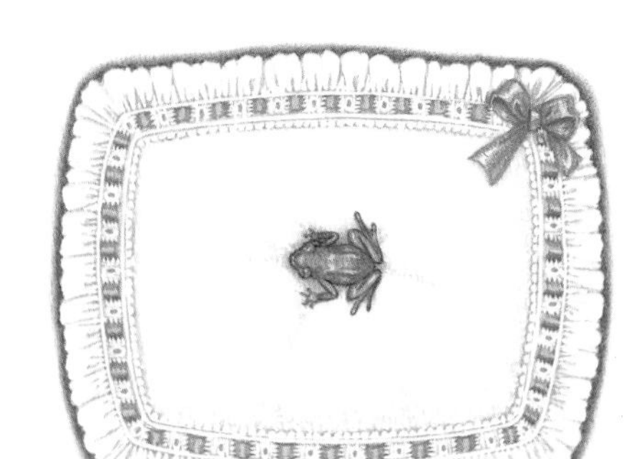

When he had eaten as much as he could, the frog said, "Now I am tired. Pray carry me upstairs and put me on your own little bed."

The princess was bound by her promise to do as he asked. She picked up the frog very gingerly between her fingers, carried him upstairs, and with a shudder dropped him onto her bed. He crept up onto the pillow, and there he slept all night long. But when morning came, he jumped up and hopped down the stairs and out of the palace.

"Thank heaven!" cried the princess. "Now he has gone, and I shall see no more of him!"

But she was mistaken. That night as she sat at table, there came again that same soft slippery footstep on the stair, and that same gentle knocking at the door. Once again the princess was forced to feed the frog from her own golden plate, and take him up to her own bed to sleep.

On the third night, when again the frog visited her, the princess began to regret her promise bitterly.

But on the third morning when she awoke, she found that the frog had gone from her pillow. And there, standing at the foot of the bed, was the most handsome prince she had ever seen, gazing at her with eyes that were loving and gentle and strangely like those of the little frog.

"Dear Princess!" cried the prince. "You have broken the spell at last!"

He told her how he had been enchanted by a wicked fairy. She had changed him into a frog, and told him that he would never again take human shape unless he could find a princess who would take him from the spring and bring him home with her, feed him from her own plate, and allow him to sleep upon her bed.

"Now you have done this," cried the prince, "and I love you dearly. I want you to come with me to my own kingdom, marry me, and be my queen."

And so it happened. Next day the princess drove off with her prince in a fine golden coach drawn by six white horses, bound for the prince's own kingdom, where they were married and lived happily ever after.

~ Rapunzel ~

There once lived a man and his wife who longed for a child. But as the years went by and still there was no sign of one, they began to despair. Then one day the wife was down by the stream washing clothes when a frog put his head out of the water and told her that soon her wish would be granted.

The wife was overjoyed and hurried home to tell her husband, who immediately set about making a wooden cradle for the baby.

Now, next to the cottage where these two lived was a great, overgrown garden, which belonged to a strange old woman they hardly ever saw. People said she was a witch, and they were afraid of her.

One day the wife was peering over the wall into this garden when she saw a clump of green rampion growing there. Immediately she began to long for a taste of it, though she had never been particularly fond of it before.

"Dear husband, I must eat some rampion or die!" she told him when he came home from working in the forest. "Climb over the wall and fetch me some, I beg you."

The husband did not like the idea at all.

"It doesn't belong to us," he told her. "And as for that old woman who owns the garden,

for all we know she may be a witch, and if she catches me, what then?"

"What nonsense!" cried the wife. "Witch indeed! I must have some rampion, I tell you, or I shall die!"

And so the man, although he knew full well that the old woman *was* a witch, waited until twilight and then climbed softly over the wall and began to pull up the rampion as quickly as he could. But when he straightened up to climb back over the wall, he found himself face-to-face with the old witch herself, eyes aglitter in the gloom.

"How *dare* you climb into my garden and tear up my plants!" she cried in a terrible voice. "I have caught you red-handed, and now it will be the worse for you!"

The poor man, shaking and trembling, explained how greatly his wife had longed for the rampion, and he begged the witch to forgive him.

"Never!" she cried. "But I will make a bargain with you. Your wife is about to have a child. I will let you go free and take with you as much rampion as you like, on the condition that when the child is born *I* shall have it to bring up as my own."

The man agreed – for he was so terrified that he hardly knew what he was saying – and scrambled safely back over the wall with the stolen rampion and a heavy heart.

Soon afterward a daughter was born, and when she was only a few days old, the witch came and carried the child off with her. She gave her the name Rapunzel.

When Rapunzel was twelve years old, the witch locked her in a tall stone tower that stood in the thickest and darkest part of a great wood. It had neither staircase nor doors, only a little window in Rapunzel's own room right at the very top.

Whenever the witch wanted to enter, she would stand below and call up, "Rapunzel, Rapunzel, let down your hair!"

Rapunzel had long hair the color of gold, which she wore in braids wound about her head. When she heard the witch, she would twist her braids around a hook by the window

CL

and let them down. They fell like thick golden ropes, and the witch would climb up by them.

When Rapunzel had been in the tower for several years, it happened one day that the king's son rode by. He heard a beautiful voice singing nearby, and pushing his way through the dim green thicket, he came upon the lonely sunless tower. Rapunzel's voice drifted down from the little window, and she sang so sweetly of her loneliness that the prince longed to join her. He searched about the tower to find a door, but in vain, and in the end he was forced to ride away.

After that he would often ride in the wood and make his way to the tower. And one day, while he was hidden there among the laurel leaves, the old witch herself appeared, and he heard her call out, "Rapunzel, Rapunzel, let down your hair!"

The prince saw Rapunzel's face at the high window, he saw her lift her hands to unpin her braids, and a minute later the golden ropes of hair came tumbling to the ground. While the prince watched, the witch climbed up and disappeared through the window.

"If that is the ladder that will take me to that fair lady, then I shall try my own luck," he thought.

Next day he went at evening into the forest and came to the tower in the half darkness. He called from the shadow of the thicket in a voice as hoarse as the witch's own, "Rapunzel, Rapunzel, let down your hair!"

Then at last he was grasping the smooth warm ropes of hair and climbing upward and into the little stone room.

Rapunzel was terrified when first she saw him, for she had never seen a man before. But the prince spoke gently to her, telling how he had come each day to hear her sing and how his heart had been won by her song. When he told her that he wished to take her away and marry her, he looked so kind and handsome that she could not help thinking, "He is better by far than old Mother Gothel, and surely he will love me better."

So she put her hand in his, and said, "Yes."

"But I cannot escape without a ladder," she said. "So each time you come, you must bring with you a skein of silk. I will weave it into a ladder, and when it is long enough, then I shall climb down by it, and you can take me away on your horse."

"I will come every day," the prince promised.

"But you must be sure to come in the evening," Rapunzel told him. "Old Mother Gothel comes in the daytime, and so she will never discover you."

The prince began to visit Rapunzel every evening, and they would sit together in the twilight while Rapunzel sat and wove her silken ladder. And all would have been well for them if one day Rapunzel had not said to the witch, quite without thinking, "How is it, Mother Gothel, that you are twice as heavy to draw up as the young prince who comes at evening?"

No sooner were the words out than Rapunzel saw her mistake and clapped her hand to her mouth with a little cry. But it was too late.

"What is that you say?" cried the witch in a fury. "Wicked girl – have you deceived me?"

And she seized Rapunzel's beautiful hair in one hand and with the other snatched up a pair of shears and cut off the long braids in two fierce snips. They fell to the floor in shining coils.

Rapunzel's tears and pleas were all in vain. The merciless witch spirited her from the stone tower to a far-off wilderness, where she left her to wander all alone and fend for herself.

Then, that evening, the old witch fastened the braids to the hook by the window, and waited. Sure enough, as the light faded, the prince came riding into the thicket and she heard him call, "Rapunzel, Rapunzel, let down your hair!"

With an evil smile the witch let the long ropes fall.

The prince climbed eagerly upward, and in his joy he did not notice that the golden ropes were cold as ice between his hands. He swung over the stone sill into the little room and was face-to-face with the towering witch.

"So you've come to visit your lady love!" she shrieked. "But the pretty bird has flown, my dear, the cat has got her, and she'll sing no more, I promise you! And as for you, the cat shall scratch out *your* eyes, too! Rapunzel is gone forever, and you shall never set eyes on her again!"

At this the prince was so beside himself with grief and despair that he threw himself from the window. He fell into the dark thicket, and though he was not killed, the sharp thorns scratched out his eyes and he was left in darkness.

Alone and blind, the prince wandered the woods, living on roots and berries and lamenting the loss of his bride. Years and years went by until at last he came to that very wilderness where Rapunzel had been cast by the witch and where she was still living.

As he went in darkness, he heard a sweet voice singing and knew instantly that he had found Rapunzel. He called her name out loud.

Rapunzel came running to him and fell into his arms, weeping. Two of her warm tears fell upon the prince's eyes. In that moment he could see as well as ever before, and the very first thing he saw with his new eyes was Rapunzel's face.

Then he took her away to his own kingdom, where they were welcomed with great rejoicing and married at last, to live long and happily together.

~ Snow-white and Rose-red ~

There was once a poor widow who lived in a lonely cottage. In the garden were two rose trees, and one of them bore white flowers and the other red. She also had two daughters, and one was called Snow-white and the other Rose-red.

The children were so fond of each other that they went everywhere together. When Snow-white said, "We will not leave each other," Rose-red would answer, "Never so long as we live," and their mother would add, "What one has she must share with the other."

And that was how it was. In summer they ran about the forest alone, and no harm ever came to them. On winter evenings when the snow fell, the mother would read aloud. The two girls listened as they sat and sewed. By them lay a white lamb, and above them perched a white dove.

One evening there came a knock at the door. The mother said, "Quick, Rose-red, open the door. It must be a traveler seeking shelter."

But when Rose-red opened the door, she saw not a man but a great black bear.

Rose-red screamed, the lamb bleated, the dove fluttered, and Snow-white hid under the bed. But the bear said, "Do not be afraid, I will do you no harm. I am half-frozen and only want to warm myself a little." "Poor bear," said the mother. "Lie down by the fire, but take care you do not burn your coat."

So out the girls came and fetched a broom and knocked the snow out of the bear's thick

CL

fur, and he stretched himself by the fire and growled contentedly. The lamb and dove came near him and were not afraid.

Soon the children began to play games with their clumsy guest. They climbed all over him and rolled him about and beat him with a stick until he cried:

"Snowy-white, Rosey-red,
Will you beat your lover dead?"

The bear stayed all night by the fire, and then at dawn he shambled over the snow into the forest. After that he came every evening at the same time; the door was never locked until he came. When it was spring and everywhere was green, the bear said one morning, "Now I must go away into the forest, to guard my treasures from the wicked dwarfs. In winter when the ground is frozen, they are forced to stay down below. But when the sun has warmed the earth, they come to pry and steal!"

The girls were sorry to see him go and often wandered in the forest hoping that they might meet him. Then one day they did find someone, but it was not the bear. It was a dwarf with a withered face and red eyes and a snow-white beard a yard long. The end of the beard was trapped in the crevice of a fallen tree, and the dwarf was jumping up and down trying to free it. When he saw the children, he called, "Why do you stand there? Do something! Help me!"

The girls tried very hard, and all the while he scolded them and called them names. In the end Snow-white took out her scissors and cut off the end of the dwarf's beard.

The minute he was free, the dwarf snatched up a bag of gold that lay nearby. Instead of thanking them, he said, "Stupid geese! Cutting off my fine beard! Bad luck to you!" And off he went, still grumbling.

Soon after that Snow-white and Rose-red were by a stream when they saw something like a large grasshopper jumping by the water. They ran to it and found it was the dwarf. The dwarf had been fishing, and his beard was caught in the line. A fish twice as big as the dwarf was pulling the line – and would soon have pulled him into the water.

Out came the scissors and again, *snip*!

Off came part of the beard.

The dwarf said not a word of thanks for his rescue.

"Dolts! Toadstools! Now you have spoiled my beard!"

He snatched up a sack of pearls that lay among the rushes and ran off.

A third time Rose-red and Snow-white met the dwarf. This time he had been caught up in the claws of an eagle and was screaming in terror. The girls ran and took tight hold of him. They pulled until at last the eagle let him go.

"Clumsy things!" yelled the dwarf. "You have dragged at my brown coat and torn it!"

He grabbed a sack of precious stones and scuttled off.

The two girls went on, but in the evening they passed the same place again. There was the dwarf, who had emptied out his bag of precious stones to count and gloat over them. The jewels glittered and shone in the evening sun. The dwarf saw the girls, and his

ashen face glowed red with rage. "Why do you stand gaping there?" he cried.

Just then there came a loud growling, and out of the forest lumbered a great black bear. The dwarf sprang back in fright and begged the bear to spare him.

"Take these two wicked girls instead! They're plump and tender morsels! Eat them!"

The bear gave the wicked creature a single blow with his paw. The dwarf did not move again. The girls were terrified and were going to run off when the bear said, "Snow-white and Rose-red, do not be afraid!"

As he spoke, the bearskin fell off, and there stood a handsome man, clothed all in gold.

"I am a king's son," he said. "I was bewitched by that wicked dwarf, who has stolen all my treasures. I had to run about the forest as a bear until I was freed by his death. Now he has his well-deserved punishment."

Snow-white was married to him and Rose-red to his brother, and they divided between them the treasure the dwarf had heaped in his dark cave. The old mother lived happily with her children for many years. She took the two rose trees with her. They stood before her window, and every year bore beautiful roses, white and red.

~Hansel and Gretel~

There was once a poor woodcutter who lived with his second wife and his two children at the edge of a great forest. He was so very poor that often there was no dinner, or supper either, and at last the day came when there was no food left in the pantry but a single loaf of bread.

That night his wife said, "It is no use, husband. You cannot make a living for four of us with your ax. If there were only two of us, then we might manage."

"Aye," agreed her husband. "What is to become of us?"

"I'll tell you," said the woman. "Tomorrow we must take the children deep into the forest and leave them there. We can make a fire and sit them by it with a crust of bread, and then make our way home without them."

"Never!" cried the man. "We cannot do such a thing!"

On and on through the night she nagged and worried until at last the man agreed to her plan.

Hansel and Gretel were lying awake in the next room because they could not sleep for hunger. When Gretel heard what their father and stepmother were plotting, she began to cry bitterly, muffling her sobs under the blanket.

"Don't cry, Gretel," said Hansel stoutly. "I will take care of you. We shall come safely home again, I promise."

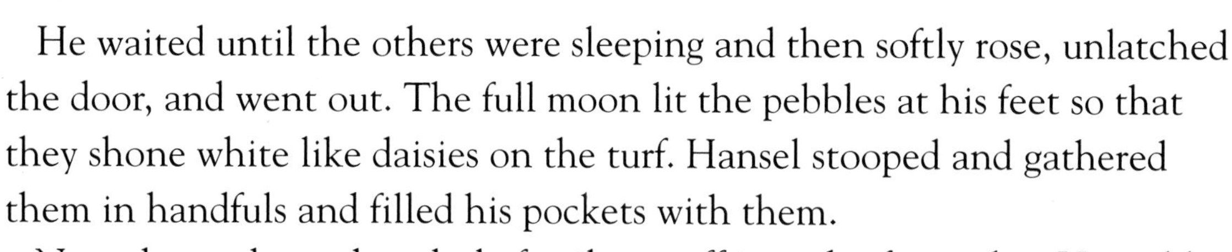

He waited until the others were sleeping and then softly rose, unlatched the door, and went out. The full moon lit the pebbles at his feet so that they shone white like daisies on the turf. Hansel stooped and gathered them in handfuls and filled his pockets with them.

Next day at dawn the whole family set off into the forest, but Hansel lagged behind. His father called over his shoulder, "Hurry, Hansel, why are you dawdling?"

"I'm saying good-bye to my white cat, who sits on the roof," replied Hansel.

"That's no cat!" his stepmother told him. "It's the sun shining on the wet roof!"

Hansel kept behind, nonetheless, because what he was really doing was dropping a pebble now and then along their way. His pockets were nearly empty when at last their father said, "We will stop here and make a fire."

Then the stepmother gave the children a crust of bread each and said, "Wait here by the fire. Your father and I are going to work nearby."

Hansel and Gretel said nothing, but sat by the fire and looked at each other. They waited for a long time, and every now and then they thought they heard the sound of an ax swinging. But it was really a loose branch that was blowing in the wind against the bark of another tree.

It began to grow dark. Hansel and Gretel ate their crusts of bread and gathered more sticks. Soon there was only one little ring of light left in the whole forest, about their own fire. The wild beasts howled in the darkness beyond. Gretel began to cry.

"Don't cry," said Hansel, putting his arm about her shoulders. "Soon the moon will be up, and then you'll see!"

Slowly the moon rose above the forest trees. Hansel stood and pointed down to the pebbles he had thrown from his pocket.

"See how they shine!" cried Gretel.

All the way home the stones shone in a silver trail before them, bright as new coins.

"Where have you been, you bad children?" cried their stepmother when they arrived

home at dawn. She behaved just as if it were all *their* fault. But Hansel and Gretel wisely said nothing at all. They could tell that their father was pleased to see them.

Things went on much as before for several months, when again the family fell on hard times and only a single stale loaf stood in the larder. That night Hansel and Gretel, lying awake in the dark, heard their stepmother plotting. At first their father would not listen, but in the end he had to give in and agree that the next day they would leave the children in the forest again. As soon as the parents fell asleep, Hansel got up. But this time the door was locked, so he had to go back to bed and think of another plan.

"Don't worry," he told his sister. "I shall think of something."

Next day, before they left for the forest, their stepmother gave them each a crust of bread. And again, as they went on their way, Hansel lagged behind and his father called out, "Why are you dawdling? Hurry up!"

Hansel replied, "I'm only looking at the white dove that is sitting on the roof to say good-bye!"

"That's no dove!" cried the stepmother. "It's the sun shining on the wet roof!"

But what Hansel was really doing was breaking his crust into crumbs and dropping them now and then to mark their way, as he had done with the pebbles.

This time Hansel and Gretel were not so frightened, because they had found their own way back once and thought that they could do it again. They sat by the fire and waited until the moon came up, then Hansel went in search of his trail of crumbs. But the thousand hungry birds of the forest had come down and eaten them up, every single one. The path toward home had gone.

Gretel began to cry, but Hansel tried to appear braver than he felt. He said, "Lie by the fire and go to sleep. Soon it will be morning and we shall easily find our way home."

They lay down and fell asleep. In the morning they set off, and Hansel was sure they were going the right way because he remembered a clump of silver birches they had passed

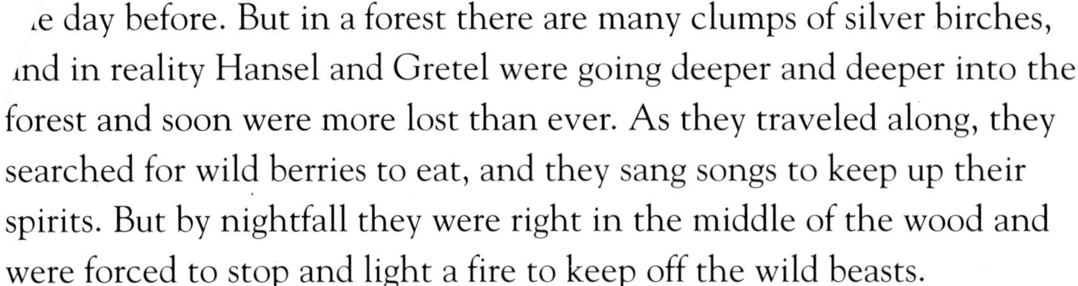

the day before. But in a forest there are many clumps of silver birches, and in reality Hansel and Gretel were going deeper and deeper into the forest and soon were more lost than ever. As they traveled along, they searched for wild berries to eat, and they sang songs to keep up their spirits. But by nightfall they were right in the middle of the wood and were forced to stop and light a fire to keep off the wild beasts.

Next day the two children set bravely off again, but by now they were so tired and hungry that they could hardly walk.

"It's no use, brother!" cried Gretel at last. "I can go no farther!"

Hansel did not hear her. He was pointing ahead to something he could glimpse through the trees, and pulling at his sister's hand, he began to hurry toward it. They both stopped and stood staring.

It was a little house with walls of gingerbread, a roof of cake, and windows of frosted sugar. Hansel ran forward and broke off a piece of the roof. "Food!" he cried, his cheeks bulging. Gretel, too, began to stuff her mouth with the rich, curranty cake. They were snapping candy from the doorposts and licking the sticky sugar from the windows when a voice came from inside the cottage:

"Tip, tap, who goes there?"

The children answered:

"Only the wind that blows through the air!"

And they carried on eating, because they had been hungry for a long time and felt as if they could devour the whole house between them. But soon a little old woman came hobbling out and cried, "Ah! What pretty little children! Are you hungry, my dears? Come along with me and I'll find you something good!"

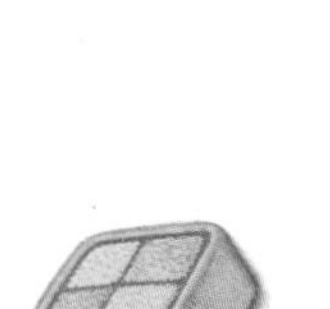

This old woman had built her house of gingerbread and candy to catch the eye of children wandering in the wood. But Hansel and Gretel did not know this, and they followed her indoors, stepping over a black cat who hissed and rose into a thin arch.

The witch (for witch she was) set out a meal of milk and pancakes and sugar and apples and nuts. Then she showed the children two little white beds into which they crept, hardly believing their luck.

In the morning the witch came and looked at them while they still slept. She smacked her lips over their rosy cheeks, muttering, “They’re a pair of dainty little morsels! Now, which is the bigger, for that one I’ll eat first!”

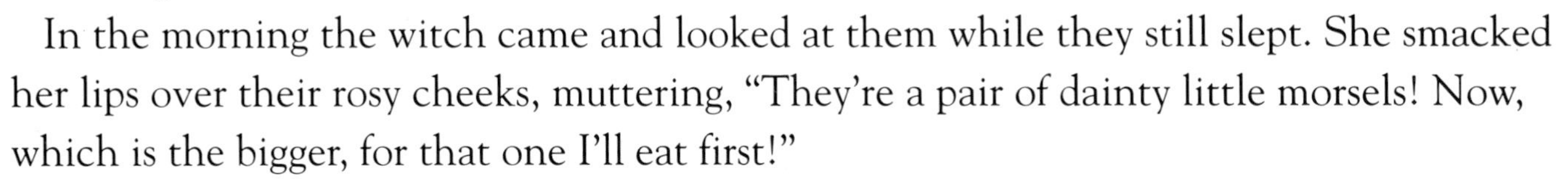

She snatched Hansel with her bony hand and dragged him into a little pen that stood in a corner of the kitchen. There she shut him up behind the grating, cackling with glee at the thought of the fine meal she would soon have. Then she went to Gretel and gave her a shake and cried, “Get up, lazy bones, and fetch some water and cook something nice for your brother. I want him fat, fat as can be, and the sooner he’s fat, the sooner I can eat him for my dinner!”

Gretel began to cry when she saw Hansel in his cage, but she was forced to obey the wicked witch and cook him a thick rich stew full of potatoes and noodles.

“Fatter and fatter,” nodded the old witch, peering at him as he ate.

Every day Hansel was given three big meals, while Gretel herself had next to nothing

and was soon as skinny as the witch's cat. But Hansel grew fatter and fatter. The witch herself could not see very well, because all witches have red eyes that are very shortsighted. So each day she went to the cage and commanded, "Hansel, put out your finger so I can feel how fat you are!"

But Hansel, instead of putting out his finger, would push an old knucklebone between the bars of the cage.

"A pity, a pity, not fat enough yet!" the old woman would grumble, and give the cat a kick.

At last, one day, the witch felt the knucklebone for the fiftieth time and suddenly cried, "Today! I'll have him today, fat or lean! Light the fire, girl, and put water in the pan! I'll have Hansel for my dinner, with plenty of gravy to dip the bread in!"

Poor Gretel got down on her knees and lit the fire. Hansel sat shaking with fear inside his little cage.

"We'll bake first," said the old witch. "I'll knead the dough while you creep into the oven and see if it's hot enough."

She gave Gretel a push, then stood by so that when the girl had crept into the oven, she could slam the door and cook her, too, along with the bread.

"I don't see how to get in," said Gretel, who knew very well what would happen to her if she did climb in.

"Goose!" shrieked the witch. "Simpleton! Anyone could do it! Look – like this!"

She hobbled to the oven and put her head and shoulders right inside, and Gretel came up behind her and gave a great push. *Bang* went the oven door! The witch was inside! She let out such a howl that the ribby cat gave one last sizzling hiss and shot out of the cottage and away into the forest, his tail stiff as a poker with fright. Hansel stamped his feet with joy and rattled at the bars of the cage.

"Hurrah!" he cried. "Bravo! The old witch is dead and roasted! Serves her right! And good riddance to the old cat, too! Let me out now, let me out!"

Gretel ran and undid the latch, and they both danced around laughing and crying – one fat and the other thin, but both merry as larks to be free again.

In the cottage they found chests full of treasure. Hansel stuffed his pockets with pearls and precious stones. Gretel filled her apron with gold and silver pieces and then broke off a big hunk of cake from the cottage roof to last them until they were home.

Off they set, and as if by magic, this time they found the right way. By nightfall they could see their father's house in the distance, with a candle burning in the window.

Their father was overjoyed to see them alive and well, and told them that their stepmother was now dead.

"But if you will forgive me, the three of us can live together again, and whatever we have in the world, even if it is but a crust, we will share it."

"Then we'll start by sharing this!" cried Gretel. She let her apron drop, and all the gold and silver went raining down to the earthen floor under her father's astonished eyes. Hansel turned his pockets inside out, and rubies and pearls flew to all four corners of the hut.

"Praise be!" cried the good woodman. "Now we are rich! And since you are here, we can be happy!"

And so they were, ever after.

~Little Red Riding Hood~

Once upon a time there was a little girl who lived with her mother by the edge of a big forest. The girl's mother had made her a cloak and hood of bright red wool, and she wore it so often that she became known as Little Red Riding Hood.

One day her mother called her and said, "Your grandmother is not well. I have made some little cakes and put them in this basket, and there's a pat of butter and some newly laid eggs. I want you to take them to her and see how she is. But mind you go straight there and back and don't go off the path."

Little Red Riding Hood was very fond of her grandmother and gladly set off along the path that led to her cottage. It was a fine, sunny day and the wild flowers were blooming all about, so after a while Little Red Riding Hood thought, "It's early in the day, and there's plenty of time. And I would have to step only a *little* way off the path to pick some of these flowers. I could take them to Grandmother to make her feel better."

So she wandered off the path and began picking flowers. She was soon deep in the wood.

In the distance she could hear the blows of the woodcutters' axes and sometimes their voices, singing while they worked. But she didn't hear the Wolf of the Wood, who was lurking nearby, spying from behind a tree.

"This looks a juicy morsel," thought he. "But I dare not eat her here – the woodcutters are too close. I will speak to her and find out where she is going."

So he came out from behind the tree and said as softly as he could, "Good day, little girl. Are you walking the same way I am? Perhaps I could carry your basket for you so that you can pick flowers more easily?"

"Thank you kindly, sir," replied Little Red Riding Hood. "But I am going to my grandmother's cottage, just along the path to the other side of the wood. And as I'm nearly there, I won't put you to any trouble."

"Good day, then," said the wolf politely. "I hope that we shall meet again soon."

He hoped so very much indeed, and Little Red Riding Hood had not noticed the wicked glint in his eye when she told him where she was going.

She picked another handful of buttercups and daisies, then returned to the path that led toward her grandmother's cottage.

When she knocked at the door, a hoarse voice called out, "Lift the latch, and the door will open. Come right in, my dear!"

Little Red Riding Hood lifted the latch and went in. She saw her grandmother lying in bed wearing a big frilled nightcap, with the blankets pulled up to her chin.

"I'm sorry to find you in bed, Grandmother," said she. "I've brought you some cakes that Mother has baked, and a pat of butter and some newly laid eggs. And here are some flowers I picked myself to cheer you up and make your room look bright."

The wolf (for the wolf it was, under the frilled lace nightcap) told her to put the food in the pantry and to arrange the flowers in a vase.

"Now you must sit beside me and rest," he said when Little Red Riding Hood had finished.

She went up close to the bed, thinking how strangely her grandmother had changed, now that she was sick.

"Oh, Grandmother, what great ears you have!" she said.

"All the better to hear you with, my dear," said the wolf.

"Oh, Grandmother, what great eyes you have," said Little Red Riding Hood.

"All the better to see you with, my dear," replied the wolf.

"Oh, Grandmother, what great arms you have," cried Little Red Riding Hood.

"All the better to hug you with, my dear," said the wolf, and he stretched them out toward her.

But Little Red Riding Hood stepped quickly back and gasped, "Oh, Grandmother, what great *teeth* you have!"

"The better to eat you with!" cried the wolf, and he sprang up from the bed

to devour her. But just then a wasp flew through the open window and stung him on the nose. The wolf let out a great yowl, and as he howled the door opened and an arrow flew straight in and pierced the wicked wolf through and through.

Little Red Riding Hood turned and saw, standing in the doorway with his bow in hand, the Green Archer, who was keeper of the forest for the king.

"I saw you talking with the wicked wolf, little maid," he said, "and came to save you. Your grandmother is safe and sound at my house. It was Puck the fairy who changed himself into the wasp and made the wolf howl as a signal for me to shoot my arrow. For I don't like little girls to be eaten up, even when they do disobey their mothers and wander away from the path and speak with wolves."

Little Red Riding Hood's face turned so red that it almost matched her cloak.

"I shall never do so again," she promised. And she never did.

Snow White ~and the~ Seven Dwarfs

A queen sat sewing by the window one day when the snow was falling. She lifted her head to see a raven walking on the white lawns, and as she did so, she pricked her finger. A drop of blood fell, and in that moment the queen made a wish.

"I wish that I might have a little daughter, and that her skin might be white as snow, her lips red as blood, and her hair black as a raven's wing."

She spoke the wish out loud, and when she had finished, the raven spread his black wings and flew off into the swirling snow.

Not long afterward a daughter was born to the king and queen, and the queen, remembering her wish, called the child Snow White. And as she grew older, her skin was white as snow, her lips were red as blood, and her hair shone like a raven's wing.

After a few years the queen died and the king married again. His new wife was beautiful but proud. She would gaze and gaze at herself in the magic glass that hung in her room, and say to it:

"Mirror, mirror, on the wall,
Who is the fairest of us all?"

Then the glass would answer:

"Pale as the moon, bright as a star,
Thou art the fairest, Queen, by far!"

And the queen would smile at her reflection in the cold glass.

But Snow White grew more and more beautiful each day, and when she was seven years old, she was even fairer than the queen herself.

The magic mirror could not tell a lie, and so when next the Queen asked it,

"Mirror, mirror, on the wall,
Who is the fairest of us all?"

the reply came:

"Fair as the day, O Queen, you are,
But Snow White is lovelier by far!"

At this the queen turned white with rage. She sent for a huntsman and told him to take Snow White deep into the forest and kill her. But when the huntsman drew his knife to plunge it into her heart, Snow White began to cry and beg for her life. The huntsman, remembering his own children at home, slowly let the knife fall.

"Run as far off as you can," he told her. "If ever you return, we shall both lose our lives."

Then he turned and left her, and on his way back to the palace he killed a fawn and cut out its heart to take back to the queen, pretending it was Snow White's.

Now Snow White was alone in the dim green forest. As she ran, the brambles clutched at her dress like live hands and the sharp stones cut into her feet. But the wild animals let

her pass without harming her, and she ran and ran all day until it was evening. Then, at dusk, she came upon a little house, the first she had seen all day. Because she was so tired, she went inside to rest. Everything was very small – and yet neat and clean as could be. There was a small table set out with a white cloth and seven little plates and seven little loaves and seven little glasses with wine in them. By the wall were seven little beds, neatly made, with not a wrinkle on them.

Snow White was so hungry that she went right around the table, taking a little nibble from each loaf, a forkful of vegetables from each plate, and a sip of wine from each glass.

Then, because she was so tired after her day in the forest, she went to the row of beds and tried first one and then another until she found one that was comfortable. She lay down and went straight to sleep.

Soon afterward the owners of the house came home. They were seven dwarfs, who worked all day deep in the mountainside with picks and shovels, digging for gold and precious stones. In they came and took off their boots and left them in a row by the door. Then they lit the lamps and saw at once that things were not as they had left them.

"Who has been sitting in my chair?" asked the first.

"Who has been using my fork?" asked the second.

"Who has been nibbling my bread?" asked the third.

"Who has been picking at my vegetables?" asked the fourth.

"Who has been drinking out of my glass?" asked the fifth.

"Who has been cutting with my knife?" asked the sixth.

"And who has been eating off my plate?" asked the seventh.

Then one of them went over to his bed and saw a dent in the cover and he cried, "Someone has been sitting on my bed!"

Then all the rest ran up to their beds, crying, "And mine! And mine!" until the seventh

dwarf went to *his* bed and found Snow White herself, fast asleep.

"*Sssssh!*" he hissed loudly to the others. "*Sssssh*! Come and look!"

All seven dwarfs crowded around the bed, whispering and nudging one another and fixing their eyes on Snow White's beautiful face.

"What a lovely child!" they whispered. "We mustn't wake her!"

So all through the night the seven dwarfs took turns watching Snow White's bedside, an hour each. When she awoke and saw the seven dwarfs, Snow White was frightened and covered her eyes. But they spoke gently to her and asked her name and how she had come there alone through the thick forest. Snow White told them her story, and when she had finished, the first dwarf asked, "Can you cook and sew and spin? Can you dust and sweep and kindle fires? Can you knit and bake, and can you trim a lamp?"

Snow White could do all these things, because her stepmother had kept her hard at work at home. And so the dwarfs said that she could stay with them and look after the house while they went off each day to dig for gold and silver in the mountains.

Each day before they set off in the gray dawn, the dwarfs would warn Snow White, "Take care to let no one in. One day the queen will find out where you are and try to harm you."

All this time the queen had thought Snow White was dead, and was so sure that she was now the most beautiful in the land that she had not troubled to use her magic mirror. But one day, when she had nothing else to do, she went and sat before it, smiled at her reflection, and asked:

"Mirror, mirror, on the wall,
Who is the fairest of us all?"

And the glass answered:

"Queen, thou art fairest here, I hold,
But in the forest and over fell
Snow White with the seven dwarfs doth dwell,
And she is fairer, a thousandfold!"

At this the queen went mad with hate and envy. She lifted her arm to shatter the mirror into a thousand pieces. But her arm fell and she thought, "No. It is not the mirror I must destroy, but Snow White!"

Next day the queen stained her face brown, dressed in rags like a pedlar woman, and set off into the forest to the cottage of the seven dwarfs. There she stood beneath the window, with her big hat shading her face, and called out, "Wares to sell! Wares to sell!"

Snow White put her head out of the window. "Good day," she said. "What have you to sell?"

"Pretty trinkets," replied the wicked queen. "And colored laces for your waist!"

She held up one of beautiful scarlet silk, dangling it under Snow White's eyes so that she thought, "Surely I may let this pedlar in? She seems kind and honest, and has such pretty things!"

She opened the door and let the queen in.

"Gracious, child!" the queen cried. "How badly your dress is laced! Here, let *me* do it with this pretty scarlet lace, and you shall have it for a penny!"

Snow White stood quite still while the pedlar threaded the new red lace with nimble fingers. But the wicked queen pulled the laces tighter and tighter and tighter until all the breath was squeezed out of Snow White's body and she fell to the floor and lay there as if she were dead.

"That's the end of *you* and your beauty!" cried the spiteful queen, who hastened back toward the palace.

When the dwarfs came back and found Snow White lying lifeless on the floor, they guessed at once what had happened. One of them seized a knife and cut the scarlet lace. At once Snow White drew in a great sigh and began to breathe again. The dwarfs gave a shout of joy, and next day when they set off in the mists for the mountains, they begged her to take care and be on the watch for the wicked queen.

That very morning the queen herself rose early and went to the magic mirror.

"Mirror, mirror, on the wall,
Who is the fairest of us all?"

When the mirror gave the same answer as before, the queen could not speak for anger. In terrible silence she dressed in a disguise, a different one, and took up a tray of bright combs. She painted one of the combs with deadly poison. Then she set off to the dwarfs' house, where she knocked on the door and cried, "Fine wares to sell! Fine wares to sell!"

Again Snow White looked through the window, and said, "I cannot open the door – I dare not! I have promised to let no one in!"

"There is no need to open the door," replied the queen. "Just look at my beautiful combs. See, I will pass one up for you to try."

She picked out a carved comb of finest ivory. Snow White took it from her and put it into her hair. No sooner had she done so than she fell to the floor in a deadly swoon.

"There you may lie!" cried the wicked queen and went on her way.

Luckily, that day the dwarfs came home from the mountains early and found Snow White before she was quite dead. They gently took the poisoned comb from her hair, and after a time she opened her eyes and sat up. When she told them what had happened, they warned her yet again to beware, and again Snow White promised that she would.

That very night the queen went back to her magic mirror. When she received the same reply as before and knew that Snow White must still be living, she shivered and shook with rage. She pointed her long white finger into the mirror, and it pointed back at her.

"Snow White shall die!" she cried. "Even if it costs *my* life!"

All night long she secretly worked at a poisoned apple. One side of it was rosy and shining, the other clear and green. Whoever took a bite from the red side was sure to die.

At dawn the queen went gliding out to the woods dressed as a peasant's wife. When she came to the dwarfs' house, she knocked – and Snow White put her head out of the window.

"I cannot open the door," she said. "The dwarfs have made me promise not to."

"Very well," said the old woman. "It doesn't matter to me whether you do or not. But perhaps you'd like this pretty apple as a present before I go?"

Snow White shook her head.

"What is the matter?" asked the peasant woman. "Do you think that it is poisoned? Silly girl – see, watch me!"

She turned the green side of the apple to her lips and bit into it.

"There!" said she. "If it were poisoned, do you think *I* should have eaten it? Here, take the rest and eat it!"

Snow White longed for the shining red apple with its juicy flesh. She took it from the old woman, bit into the rosy skin, and next minute fell to the ground.

"This time nothing shall save her!" cried the queen, who hastened back to the castle and stood before the magic mirror. At last it gave her the answer she wanted:

"Thou art the fairest, Queen, by far!"

When the dwarfs came home in the twilight, laden with gold, they found Snow White lying there on the floor. They lifted her up, splashed her face with cold water, and did everything they could think of to bring her back to life. It was in vain. Snow White's eyelids never flickered, not the faintest breath floated from her lips. For seven days and

CL

seven nights they watched by her side, but there was not the least stir of life. For all that, Snow White was still so beautiful that they could hardly bring themselves to believe that she was really dead.

"We can't bury her in the cold ground!" they cried. So they made a coffin of glass and placed her in it and wrote her name on it in gold letters. They carried the coffin to the mountainside, and one of the dwarfs always sat by it and watched, day and night. And all the birds of the air came singly out of the sky to lament the death of Snow White: the owl, the raven, and at last the dove.

Snow White lay many years on the bare mountainside, and still she seemed only to sleep. Her lips were red as blood, her skin was white as snow, and her hair was black as a raven's wing – just as they had been in life.

It happened one day that the son of a king came riding by and saw Snow White within her glass walls. He read the gold lettering and learned her name, and that she was the daughter of a king.

"Give her to me!" he begged the dwarfs. But they all shook their heads and refused to let her go.

"I will give you gold and treasure," pleaded the prince.

Again they refused. "We will not give her up for all the treasure in the world!"

"Then I shall stay here on the mountain all my days looking at Snow White," said the prince. "I cannot live without her."

At this the dwarfs pitied him and could not deny him what he asked. They lifted the coffin, and as they did so, the piece of poisoned apple fell from Snow White's lips. She opened her eyes, lifted her head, and cried in astonishment, "What's happening?"

The prince, overjoyed, lifted her from the coffin and told her the story of how she had been poisoned by the wicked queen and had lain like one dead for more than seven years.

"But now you have come to life again," he said. "And I love you better than all the

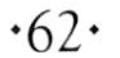

world. Come with me to my father's kingdom and marry me!"

And so Snow White said farewell to the seven dwarfs and went with the prince to his father's castle, where a great feast was prepared for their wedding.

Among the guests invited was Snow White's wicked stepmother. She dressed herself in her finest clothes, and when she was ready, she stood before the magic mirror and smiled proudly.

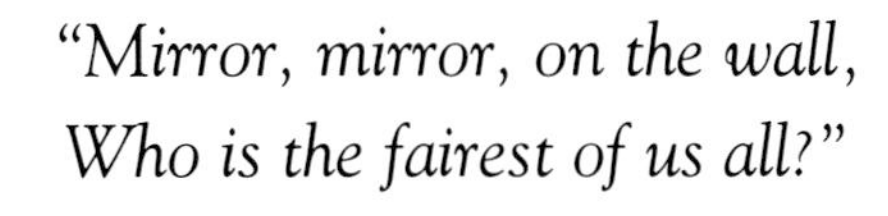

"Mirror, mirror, on the wall,
Who is the fairest of us all?"

Then the glass replied:

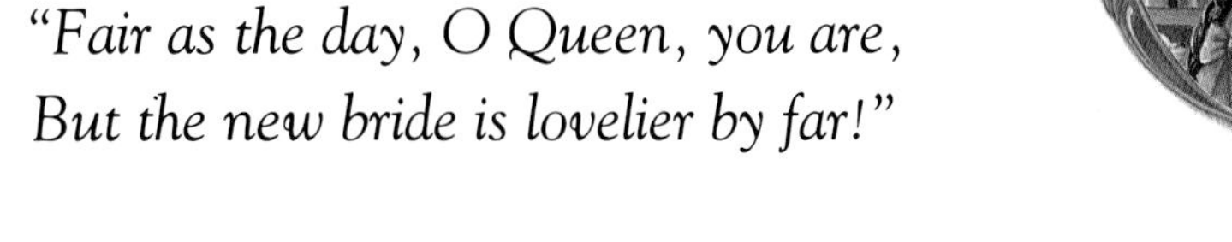

"Fair as the day, O Queen, you are,
But the new bride is lovelier by far!"

At this the queen's fury was so great that she lifted her jeweled hand and struck the glass, breaking it into a thousand pieces. Then she went out and rode to the wedding so that she could see with her own eyes this bride who was even more beautiful than herself.

And when she went into the hall and saw that the bride was none other than Snow White, she flew into such a passion of hate and envy that her heart burst and she fell down dead.

But Snow White and the prince were married that day and lived and reigned happily ever after.